Legs

Written by Jo Windsor

Legs are
for walking.

Legs are
for jumping.

Look at the insect.
The insect is jumping.

legs

8

legs

Index

▬▬ Guide Notes

> **Title:** Legs
>
> **Stage:** Emergent – Magenta
>
> **Genre:** Nonfiction (Expository)
> **Approach:** Guided Reading
> **Processes:** Thinking Critically, Exploring Language, Processing Information
> **Written and Visual Focus:** Photographs (static images), Index, Labels
> **Word Count:** 36

FORMING THE FOUNDATION

Tell the children that this book is about the different ways animals and people can move.
Talk to them about what is on the front cover. Read the title and the author.
Focus the children's attention on the index and talk about what they will find out in this book.
"Walk" through the book, focusing on the photographs and talk about the people and the animals and the way they are moving.

Read the text together.

THINKING CRITICALLY
(sample questions)

After the reading
• What do you think we can do with our legs that animals can't?
• Some animals do not have legs. How do you think they move around?

EXPLORING LANGUAGE
(ideas for selection)

Terminology
Title, cover, author, photographs

Vocabulary
Interest words: walking, turtle, jumping, insect, running, horse
High-frequency words: are, for, look, at, the, is